D0122294

Apr 17

CARTOON NETWORK BOOKS
Penguin Young Readers Group
An Imprint of Penguin Random House LLC

Photo credits: pages 1, 2, 38: (explosion) © Thinkstock/jakkapan21; page 9: (chem lab)
© Thinkstock/Ingram Publishing; pages 16, 36: (ocean) © Thinkstock/IakovKalinin; page 16: (beach)
© Thinkstock/Purestock; pages 11, 63, 69: (blue explosion) © Thinkstock/Wavebreakmedia Ltd; page 21: (black hole)
© Thinkstock/3quarks; page 22: (pink eye) © Thinkstock/offstocker; page 24: (Newton) © Thinkstock/GeorgiosArt;
pages 28, 29: (night sky) © Thinkstock/standret; pages 35, 38, 39: (Earth) © Thinkstock/Stocktrek Images;
pages 36, 37: (sky) © Thinkstock/AlinaMD; page 40: (feldspar) © Thinkstock/alex5248, (mica)
© Thinkstock/MarcelC, (quartz) © Thinkstock/ WestLight; pages 40, 41: (gemstones) © Thinkstock/VvoeVale;
pages 42, 79: (dirt) © Thinkstock/MartinLisner; page 44: (fault) © Thinkstock/semnic, (sound wave)
© Thinkstock/stefanamer; page 49: (virus) © Thinkstock/Aunt_Spray; page 61, 64: (lightning)
© Thinkstock/mishooo; page 65: (circuit board) © Thinkstock/MauMyHaT;
page 69: (bacteria) © Thinkstock/Zoonar RF

TM and © Turner Broadcasting System Europe Limited, Cartoon Network. (s16)

Published in 2016 by Cartoon Network Books, an imprint of Penguin Random House LLC,
345 Hudson Street, New York, New York 10014. Manufactured in China.

ISBN 9781101995143   10 9 8 7 6 5 4 3 2 1

THE AMAZING WORLD OF GUMBALL

GUMBALL'S Guide to SCIENCE

by Kiel Phegley
illustrated by Shane L. Johnson

CARTOON NETWORK BOOKS

An Imprint of Penguin Random House

TABLE OF CONTENTS

CHAPTER 1
THE SCIENTIFIC METHOD

BEFORE WE CAN START BREAKING THE BOUNDARIES OF WHAT MANKIND KNOWS, WE NEED TO COVER THE INS AND OUTS OF THE *SCIENTIFIC METHOD*.

METHOD? THAT SOUNDS A LOT LIKE RULES, WHICH SOUNDS A LOT LIKE SCHOOL. CAN'T WE JUST LOOK IT UP ON THE INTERNET?

NO WAY! THE INTERNET IS FULL OF MUMBO JUMBO (AND CAT VIDEOS). THE *SCIENTIFIC METHOD* PROVES SOMETHING IS EMPIRICALLY TRUE. IT'S THE ULTIMATE POWER!

Explore the Scientific Method with Mr. Dad!

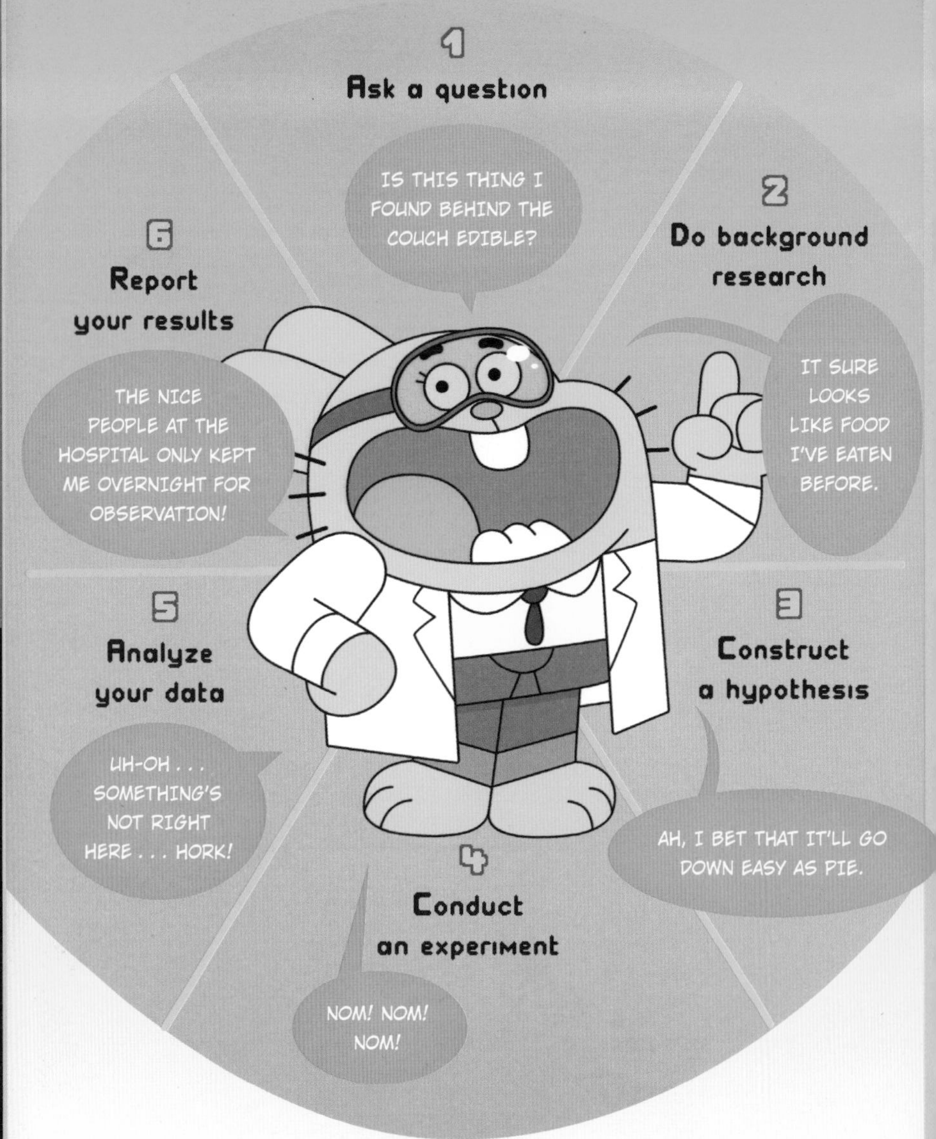

CHAPTER 2

CHEMISTRY

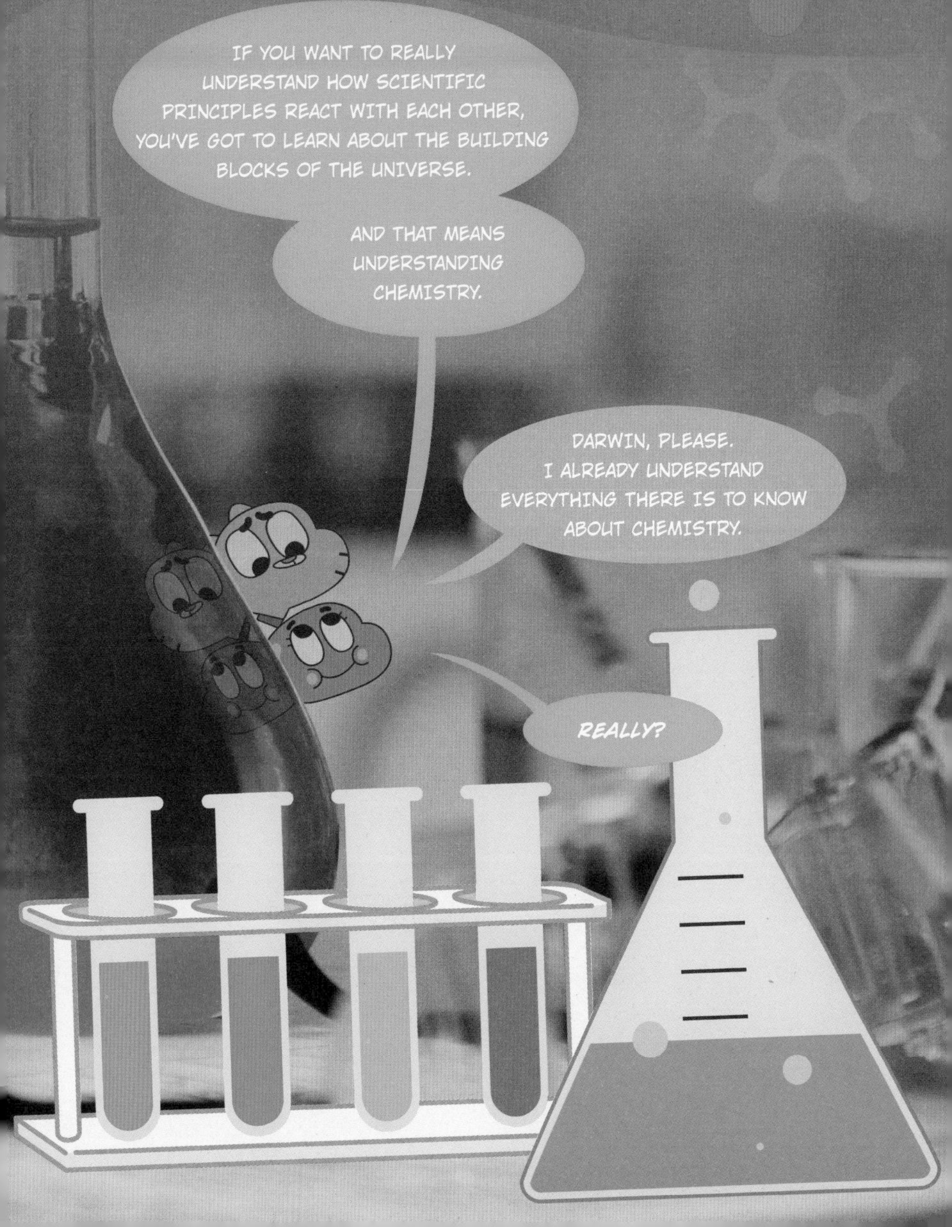

OH, HEY THERE, PENNY. WHAT'S THE GOOD WORD?

OH, GUMBALL! MY NOSE IS BURNING AND MY EYES ARE WATERING . . . I HAVE TO RUN!

MAYBE TRYING TO TRICK HER INTO LIKING YOU IS A SIGN THAT YOU'RE NOT READY TO DATE YET, GUMBALL.

HOW COULD YOU SAY THAT, YOU MONSTER!!

IT'LL BE OKAY, BUDDY. WHEN YOU LEARN ABOUT REAL CHEMISTRY, YOU LEARN THAT ALL SORTS OF THINGS YOU NEVER EXPECTED CAN GET TOGETHER. AND THAT'S ALL THANKS TO . . .

THE MIGHTY ATOM!

ATOMS ARE THE TEENY THINGS THAT WE USE IN CHEMISTRY TO MAKE ALL SORTS OF OTHER THINGS.

ATOMS ARE THE MICROSCOPIC BUILDING BLOCKS THAT MAKE UP OUR PHYSICAL REALITY. THEY'RE MADE OF A NUCLEUS (A CHEWY CENTER COMPOSED OF PROTONS AND NEUTRONS) AND CLOUDS OF ELECTRONS THAT SPIN AROUND THEM.

SERIOUSLY? HOW MUCH COOL STUFF CAN EXIST BECAUSE OF A BUNCH OF TINY, SPINNING GLOW-BALLS?

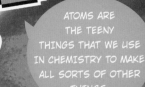

11

THE PERIODIC TABLE

ARE YOU KIDDING? WE'VE DISCOVERED 118 DIFFERENT CHEMICAL ELEMENTS! THESE REPRESENT THE BUILDING BLOCKS OF OUR WORLD!

YEAH, BUT WHEN WAS THE LAST TIME YOU REALLY NEEDED SOME TUNGSTEN?

SCIENTISTS ORGANIZE ELEMENTS IN THE PERIODIC TABLE BY THEIR ATOMIC NUMBER, WHICH IS DETERMINED BY THE NUMBER OF PROTONS IN ONE OF THEIR ATOMS.

1 H								
3 Li	4 Be							
11 Na	12 Mg							
19 K	20 Ca	21 Sc	22 Ti	23 V	24 Cr	25 Mn	26 Fe	27 Co
37 Rb	38 Sr	39 Y	40 Zr	41 Nb	42 Mo	43 Tc	44 Ru	45 Rh
55 Cs	56 Ba	57–71	72 Hf	73 Ta	74 W	75 Re	76 Os	77 Ir
87 Fr	88 Ra	89–103	104 Rf	105 Db	106 Sg	107 Bh	108 Hs	109 Mt

THE FIRST ELEMENT IS HYDROGEN, WHICH IS ALSO THE LIGHTEST.

57 La	58 Ce	59 Pr	60 Nd	61 Pm	62 Sm	63 Eu
89 Ac	90 Th	91 Pa	92 U	93 Np	94 Pu	95 Am

WHOA, THIS IS GETTING HEAVY.

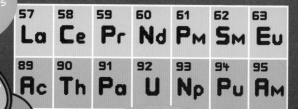

OF ELEMENTS!!!

ON THIS SIDE, THE TABLE LISTS THE SIX NOBLE GASES. THESE ARE COLORLESS, ODORLESS, AND MOST COMMONLY APPEAR BY THEMSELVES IN THE UNIVERSE.

WHEN DAD IS BY HIMSELF, HE PRODUCES A LOT OF COLORLESS GAS, BUT IT SURE ISN'T ODORLESS OR NOBLE!

					2 He
5 B	6 C	7 N	8 O	9 F	10 Ne
13 Al	14 Si	15 P	16 S	17 Cl	18 Ar

28 Ni	29 Cu	30 Zn	31 Ga	32 Ge	33 As	34 Se	35 Br	36 Kr
46 Pd	47 Ag	48 Cd	49 In	50 Sn	51 Sb	52 Te	53 I	54 Xe
78 Pt	79 Au	80 Hg	81 Tl	82 Pb	83 Bi	84 Po	85 At	86 Rn
110 Ds	111 Rg	112 Cn	113 Uut	114 Fl	115 Uup	116 Lv	117 Uus	118 Uuo

THESE TWO ROWS AT THE BOTTOM INCLUDE RARE-EARTH METALS AND MANY COMMON RADIOACTIVE ELEMENTS.

64 Gd	65 Tb	66 Dy	67 Ho	68 Er	69 Tm	70 Yb	71 Lu
96 Cm	97 Bk	98 Cf	99 Es	100 Fm	101 Md	102 No	103 Lr

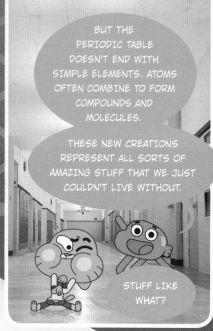

BUT THE PERIODIC TABLE DOESN'T END WITH SIMPLE ELEMENTS. ATOMS OFTEN COMBINE TO FORM COMPOUNDS AND MOLECULES.

THESE NEW CREATIONS REPRESENT ALL SORTS OF AMAZING STUFF THAT WE JUST COULDN'T LIVE WITHOUT.

STUFF LIKE WHAT?

WHEN TWO ATOMS OF HYDROGEN COMBINE WITH ONE ATOM OF OXYGEN, WE GET WATER—THE SUBSTANCE THAT MAKES UP THE MAJORITY OF OUR PLANET'S SURFACE AND OUR SQUISHY BODIES!

THIS WOULD BE COOL EXCEPT FOR THE FACT THAT CATS HATE WATER!

FORMULA: H_2O

LIFE IS A BEACH WHEN YOU COMBINE AN ATOM OF SILICON WITH TWO ATOMS OF OXYGEN TO CREATE THE COMPOUND SILICON DIOXIDE—THE MAJORITY COMPONENT OF SAND!

BUT YOU KNOW AT LEAST PART OF THIS BEACH IS SEAGULL POOP, TOO.

FORMULA: SiO_2

BUT SCIENTISTS CAN ALSO CREATE INCREDIBLY COMPLEX CHEMICAL COMPOUNDS IN THEIR LABS, LIKE ACRYLONITRILE BUTADIENE STYRENE—A KIND OF PLASTIC USED TO MAKE ALL SORTS OF STUFF, FROM BUILDING BLOCKS TO VIDEO GAMES!

FORMULA: $(C_8H_8)_x \cdot (C_4H_6)_y \cdot (C_3H_3N)_z$

IT'S... SO... BEAUTIFUL!

CHEMICAL COMPOUNDS!

INSTRUCTIONS:

Help Gumball figure out the names of these basic chemical compounds that you interact with every day.

1. CO_2

You breathe it out, and plants like Leslie breathe it in.

2. $C_{12}H_{22}O_{11}$

It's the sweetest thing in life, whether it's coating Daisy Flakes or getting mixed into chocolate chip cookies.

3. $CaCO3$

Miss Simian uses it to write your name on the board. Gumball uses it to draw a cartoon of her on the sidewalk after class.

4. $C_6H_8O_6$

Also known as ascorbic acid, it's the super-healthy stuff you need from orange juice, kale, and papaya.

5. $C_9H_8O_4$

Mrs. Mom gives Mr. Dad one of these whenever he hurts himself, and then she takes one for her headache, too.

6. $Na_2B_4O_7 \cdot 10H_2O$

This powdery substance is commonly used in household products like laundry detergent.

THEN TURN TO PAGE 79 FOR THE ANSWER!

THIS LAST ONE IS LITERALLY IMPOSSIBLE!

DO-IT-YOURSELF EXPERIMENT: CHEMICAL SLIME!

MAKE YOUR OWN TOTALLY DISGUSTING CHEMICAL COMPOUND

WHAT YOU'LL NEED:

→ Warm water
→ Measuring cups and mixing bowls
→ Classic white school glue
→ Household borax powder
  (that's chemical compound $Na_2B_4O_7 \cdot 10H_2O$)
→ Food coloring for extra-gross fun

WHAT YOU DO:

→ Combine 1/2 cup (4 ounces) of glue and 1/2 cup of water in a mixing bowl and stir.
→ Add food coloring to the mixture.
→ Pour 1 cup of water into another mixing bowl and add 1 teaspoon of borax powder. Mix thoroughly.
→ Stir glue mixture into borax solution and knead until extra slimy.

MAKE A HYPOTHESIS:

→ What do you think will happen?

TEST YOUR HYPOTHESIS:

→ Did the consistency of the slime change over time? Why do you think that is?

→ What did the food coloring do to the slime? If you use multiple colors, how does it change? For extra fun, try adding glow-in-the-dark paint to the glue mixture.

→ If you don't refrigerate your slime, it'll grow mold. Why would that be?

Science Safety Tips
with Mrs. Mom!

I MAY NOT ALWAYS BE ABLE TO STOP GUMBALL FROM JUMPING HEADFIRST INTO A POTENTIALLY DANGEROUS AND PERFECTLY SILLY SITUATION, BUT THAT DOESN'T MEAN YOU CAN'T BE SAFE.

IF YOU'RE GOING TO ATTEMPT THE EXPERIMENTS IN THIS BOOK, USE COMMON SENSE AND FOLLOW THESE BASIC SAFETY TIPS:

1. WEAR SAFETY GOGGLES AT ALL TIMES

Your eyes are important, so before you lean in to see the radical results of your experiment, keep them covered with some clear safety goggles.

2. KEEP A PARENT HANDY

Science gets pretty lame when an adult tries to do it all for you, but you should still keep a grown-up nearby in case you need any help making history.

3. READ ALL THE INSTRUCTIONS THOROUGHLY

Science is an exact science! For the best results, make sure that you set up all your experiments as outlined in the instructions, before you go off to test your own hypotheses.

CHAPTER 3
PHYSICS

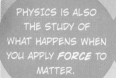

PHYSICS IS ALSO THE STUDY OF WHAT HAPPENS WHEN YOU APPLY *FORCE* TO MATTER.

THE FORCE OF *GRAVITY* HOLDS THE EARTH TOGETHER IN A SPHERE.

IT ALSO MAKES HEAVY THINGS WANT TO FALL ON YOUR HEAD. AND WHEN AN OBJECT OR GAS APPLIES FORCE OVER A GIVEN AREA, THAT'S CALLED *PRESSURE*.

AS SOON AS I GET RID OF THIS PRESSURE, I'M GOING TO FORCE YOU TO USE A BETTER EXAMPLE!

THEN THERE'S *FRICTION*—THE FORCE THAT SLOWS DOWN SOLID OBJECTS WHILE THEY SLIDE AGAINST EACH OTHER.

DRY SURFACES HAVE HIGH FRICTION, WHILE WET SURFACES, LIKE ICE, HAVE RELATIVELY LOW FRICTION.

PERSONALLY, I GET RELATIVELY LOW EVERY TIME I SLIP ON ICE.

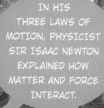

IN HIS THREE LAWS OF MOTION, PHYSICIST SIR ISAAC NEWTON EXPLAINED HOW MATTER AND FORCE INTERACT.

I DON'T KNOW, DARWIN. I TEND NOT TO TRUST OLD-TIMEY GUYS.

Exploring Newtonian Physics!

INTRO:

The laws of motion set out by Sir Isaac Newton show up in crazy ways all across the universe. Let the students of Elmore Junior High show you how!

YOU HEAR THAT? I'M STRONG ENOUGH TO MOVE THE WHOLE EARTH!

FACTOID 1:

When you run or jump, you obviously put force onto the earth. But how can there be a reaction when the ground never seems to move? Amazingly, the earth does move when you push against it. But the effect is so small that we can't perceive it.

FACTOID 2:

On earth, the force of gravity is constantly affecting the state of matter. But if you were in space and threw an object, it really would float forever unless some other force stopped its path—kind of like Carrie the ghost!

FLOATING FOREVER IN THE COLD BLACKNESS OF SPACE WOULD BE PRETTY COOL, ACTUALLY.

FACTOID 3:

Increasing the force on an object isn't the only way to speed it up. Since the earth's atmosphere provides the counter force of air resistance, reducing the drag caused by that air can make things go faster. The study of how we do this is called aerodynamics. For example, Banana Joe would probably be pretty quick if we removed his cumbersome peel.

WHAT?!? YOU BETTER NOT TRY ANYTHING FUNNY!

ALL THIS PHYSICS TALK HAS GIVEN ME AN IDEA!

FACTOID 4:

If the forces that work on an object are equal on both sides, then the object is said to be in a state of equilibrium. That's probably why Tina and Hector always tie at tug-of-war!

HOW COME I DON'T LIKE THE SOUND OF THAT?

DUDE, I'M TOTALLY COMING WITH YOU. I JUST WANTED YOU TO BE SAFE AND SECURE, BUDDY.

WHEN DO YOU THINK IT WILL...

FWOOSH!

AW, THANKS, PAL.

THE PRESSURIZED MIX IS SET. I CAN FEEL THE FIZZINESS BUILDING UP!

WAIT! THIS DOESN'T MAKE SENSE. TO ATTAIN AN ESCAPE VELOCITY STRONG ENOUGH TO PULL AWAY FROM EARTH'S GRAVITATIONAL FIELD, WE'D NEED TO BE GOING OVER 25,000 MILES PER HOUR. THERE'S NO WAY WE ACCELERATED THAT MUCH WITH JUST FIZZINESS.

WE'RE CARTOON CHARACTERS, DARWIN. DON'T YOU KNOW THAT CARTOON PHYSICS FOLLOWS A MUCH WACKIER SET OF RULES THAN THE REAL THING?

THAT'S ACTUALLY A SOLID POINT.

DO-IT-YOURSELF EXPERIMENT: POP ROCKET!

BLAST OFF FROM YOUR OWN BACKYARD

YOU MIGHT NOT BE ABLE TO BREAK FREE OF PLANET EARTH JUST YET, BUT YOU CAN STILL HAVE SOME EXPLOSIVE ROCKET FUN.

DON'T TELL THEM WHAT THEY CAN'T DO, DARWIN. ONWARD TO COSMIC GLORY!

JUST THE THOUGHT OF THOSE TABLETS IS MAKING MY STOMACH GRUMBLE. MMMMM . . . CHERRY FLAVORED!

WHAT YOU'LL NEED:

- → Any kind of plastic tube or canister with a snap-on lid, such as a mini M&Ms tube, a 35mm film canister, a pill bottle, or a clean, used-up glue stick container
- → Common "fizzy" antacid tablets from your medicine cabinet
- → Warm water
- → Some cardboard, tinfoil, and glue to make fins and a nose cone for your rocket (this cuts down the air resistance)

RICHARD, WE ARE NOT TAKING YOU TO GET YOUR STOMACH PUMPED AGAIN!

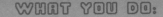

WHAT YOU DO:

→ To begin rocket prep, put on your safety goggles and make sure your container's cap is fully removable and easy to snap on quickly.

→ Take a piece of cardboard and twist it into a 1-inch cone shape, securing the shape with glue. Then glue the whole cone onto the bottom of the container, which will now be the top of your rocket.

→ For more aerodynamic features, cut small triangles of cardboard to glue as fins closer to the rocket's back (the cap end). Cover the cone and fins in tinfoil for extra reinforcement.

→ Fill your container up with water until you have about 1/2 inch of space at the top.

→ Drop in an antacid tablet and quickly snap your cap on! Then place the container cap-down on a safe surface and step back several feet.

→ Watch your rocket launch!

MAKE A HYPOTHESIS:

→ What do you think will happen?

TEST YOUR HYPOTHESIS:

→ Did the rocket launch right away? What if you tried more pieces of tablet or more water?

→ Do you think the fins and cone helped make it fly higher? Try a rocket without any and measure the height each version attains on liftoff.

POP QUIZ

NAME: <u>GUMBALL WATTERSON</u>

1. What is the chemical compound that composes over 60 percent of your body?
PIZZA!

2. The force that slows down solid objects to keep them from rubbing against each other is called what?
PRINCIPAL BROWN

3. Every solid thing in the universe is made of what?
DREAMS

4. What is the part of the scientific method where you make a prediction for your experiment?
THE HIPPOPOTAMUS

5. What are the six colorless, odorless gases on the side of the periodic table called?
FLATULENCE

THAT GUMBALL WON'T TAKE ANY OF MY QUIZZES SERIOUSLY. IF YOU EXPECT TO SURVIVE THE WRATH OF MISS SIMIAN, YOU'LL NEED TO DO A LOT BETTER ON THIS POP QUIZ THAN THAT UNSCIENTIFIC CAT!

I'M NOT A PROBLEM STUDENT. I TAKE A QUIZ, I FAIL. NO PROBLEM!

6. What are the three parts of an atom?
LARRY, MOE, AND CURLY

7. The lightest element ever is also the most common one in the universe. What is it?
PIXIE DUST

8. What speed must you reach to break free of earth's gravity?
88 MILES PER HOUR!

9. Newton's first law of motion states that an object will remain at rest or in motion until what happens?
IT GETS BORED AND PLAYS VIDEO GAMES.

Anais's Amazing Space Facts

MY BROTHERS THINK THEY'RE SO COOL RIDING A ROCKET INTO OUTER SPACE, BUT HERE ARE SOME INCREDIBLE TRUE THINGS I'VE FOUND THAT ARE WAY BETTER THAN SOME DANGEROUS STUNT.

FACTOID 1:

Many people know the story of Laika, the Russian dog who was one of the first animals in space, but there have also been other astronaut animals.

The first feline in space was a French cat named Felicette, who on October 18, 1963, made a fifteen-minute space flight on the Veronique AGI rocket.

Meanwhile, the American shuttle Skylab 3 took the first fish to space in 1973—a kind of fish called mummichog, which is also known as a mud minnow.

FACTOID 2:

What's the biggest thing in the solar system? The sun, of course! The sun makes up 99.8 percent of the mass of the solar system. It's so big that if it were hollow, you'd need one million planet Earths to fill up the inside.

FACTOID 3:

Everyone knows that in space, no one can hear you, since there's no sound. But did you know that there are smells in space? Astronauts who have returned from space walks report a scent that smells like a mixture of cooked meat and metal.

PEE-YEW! SPACE SURE IS INTERESTING, BUT I WOULDN'T WANT TO LIVE THERE.

CHAPTER 4

EARTH SCIENCE

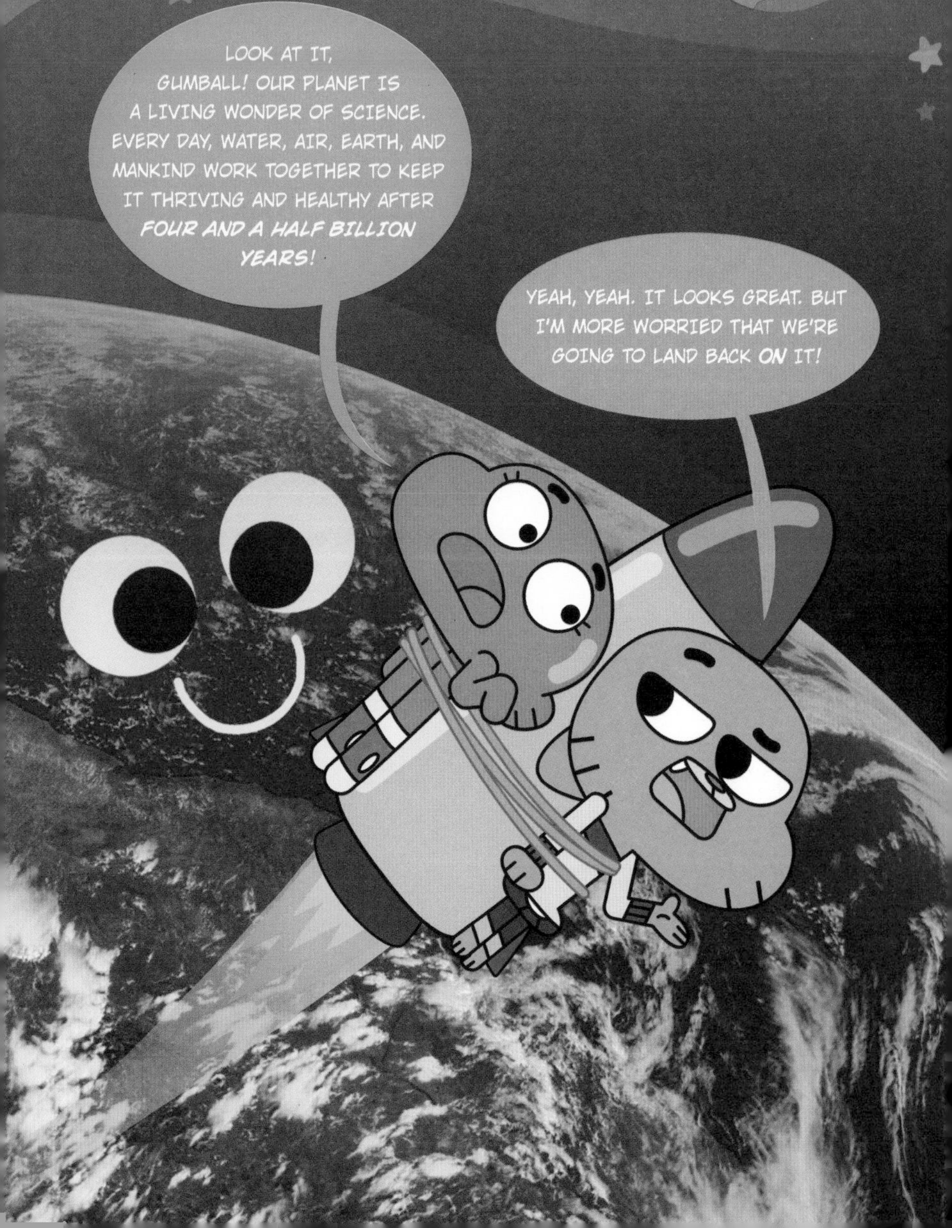

THE BOUNTIFUL BIOSPHERE OF ELMORE'S ECOSYSTEMS!

THE ENVIRONMENT OF BOTH EARTH AND ELMORE CAN BE DESCRIBED AS A *BIOSPHERE*—A ZONE WHERE ALL LIFE CAN THRIVE, THANKS TO VARIOUS ECOSYSTEMS THAT WORK TOGETHER!

THE *HYDROSPHERE* IS THE ECOSYSTEM THAT COMPRISES EARTH'S WATER SUPPLY, WHICH IS A LOT! THE SURFACE OF THE PLANET IS 71 PERCENT COVERED BY WATER.

BUT OUT OF ALL THAT, ONLY 2.5 PERCENT IS ACTUALLY DRINKABLE. AND MOST OF IT IS TRAPPED IN GLACIERS OR UNDERGROUND. WITH SO LITTLE DRINKING WATER AVAILABLE, CONSERVATION IS EXTREMELY IMPORTANT.

HYDROSPHERE

I COULD PRETTY MUCH LIVE OFF CHERRY SODA, BUT I FEEL WHERE YOU'RE COMING FROM.

KA-BOOOOOOH!

DARWIN, I THINK NEWTON MAY HAVE HAD IT RIGHT, BECAUSE WE JUST HIT THE EARTH, AND NOW THE EARTH IS DEFINITELY SPINNING.

LAWS WERE MADE TO BE FOLLOWED, GUMBALL.

BUT LOOK! LANDING ON THE MOUNTAINTOP HAS GIVEN US AN AMAZING VIEW OF ELMORE'S WHOLE BIOSPHERE!

NO OFFENSE, DARWIN, BUT ONLY YOU WOULD GET EXCITED BECAUSE YOU WERE SURROUNDED BY A BUNCH OF ROCKS.

OH, WHAT A JOY! TO THINK I NEVER GOT STRANDED MILES FROM HOME BEFORE TODAY AND MISSED THIS!

ARE YOU KIDDING, GUMBALL? ROCKS ARE AN AMAZING PART OF EARTH SCIENCE!

38

makeup of the EARTH

ALMOST EVERY ROCK YOU SEE CAME FROM THE EARTH'S CRUST—THE OUTER LAYER OF THE PLANET, WHICH IS MADE MOSTLY OF ELEMENTS LIKE OXYGEN, SILICON, ALUMINUM, AND IRON.

BUT THE CRUST IS MORE THAN EARTH'S FLAKY OUTER LAYER. IT COMBINES WITH THE FACE OF THE UPPER MANTLE TO MAKE THE LITHOSPHERE. OVER MILLONS OF YEARS, THE LITHOSPHERE HAS BEEN CONSTANTLY SHIFTING TO SHAPE OUR MODERN CONTINENTS.

CRUST
22 MILES DEEP

UPPER MANTLE
200 MILES DEEP

MANTLE
1,790 MILES DEEP

OUTER CORE
3,160 MILES DEEP

INNER CORE
3,954 MILES DEEP

NEARLY 1,800 MILES BENEATH THE EARTH'S SURFACE IS THE OUTER CORE—THE LIQUID LAYER NEAR THE CENTER, MADE MOSTLY OF IRON AND NICKEL.

BUT AT ITS FIERY HEART, THE SUPER-HOT INNER CORE ALSO CONTAINS GOLD AND PLATINUM!

THERE'S GOLD IN THEM THERE HILLS?

EVEN MORE FUN ARE THE THINGS HIDDEN WITHIN THE EARTH'S MANTLE—*ROCKS*, *MINERALS*, AND *GEMSTONES*!

GEMSTONES? GO ON . . .

THROUGHOUT EARTH'S CRUST WE CAN FIND *MINERALS*—SOLID CHEMICAL COMPOUNDS WHOSE UNIQUE ATOMIC STRUCTURE GIVES THEM A CRYSTAL SHAPE. MINERALS INCLUDE HARD AND PLAIN *FELDSPAR*, CURVY AND SHINY *QUARTZ*, AND BRITTLE AND SHARP *MICA*.

FELDSPAR

QUARTZ

MICA

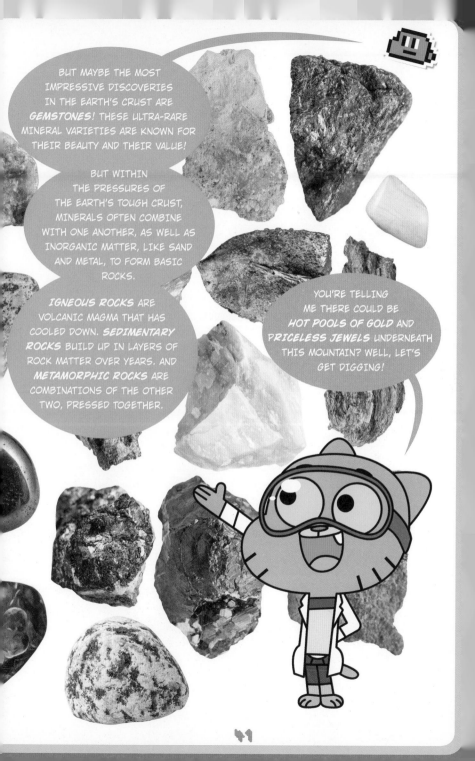

BUT MAYBE THE MOST IMPRESSIVE DISCOVERIES IN THE EARTH'S CRUST ARE *GEMSTONES!* THESE ULTRA-RARE MINERAL VARIETIES ARE KNOWN FOR THEIR BEAUTY AND THEIR VALUE!

BUT WITHIN THE PRESSURES OF THE EARTH'S TOUGH CRUST, MINERALS OFTEN COMBINE WITH ONE ANOTHER, AS WELL AS INORGANIC MATTER, LIKE SAND AND METAL, TO FORM BASIC ROCKS.

IGNEOUS ROCKS ARE VOLCANIC MAGMA THAT HAS COOLED DOWN. *SEDIMENTARY ROCKS* BUILD UP IN LAYERS OF ROCK MATTER OVER YEARS. AND *METAMORPHIC ROCKS* ARE COMBINATIONS OF THE OTHER TWO, PRESSED TOGETHER.

YOU'RE TELLING ME THERE COULD BE *HOT POOLS OF GOLD* AND *PRICELESS JEWELS* UNDERNEATH THIS MOUNTAIN? WELL, LET'S GET DIGGING!

Gumball's Gem Hunt

INSTRUCTIONS:

Dig deep into the crust of the earth with Gumball as he hunts for precious gemstones!

LIKE I WAS SAYING EARLIER, THE EARTH'S CRUST IS PART OF AN EVER-MOVING LITHOSPHERE. AND THE MOVING PARTS OF THIS SWIRLING MASS OF CRUST AND MANTLE ARE CALLED *TECTONIC PLATES.*

THE PLATES MOVE SLOWLY, BUT WHEN THEY RUB UP AGAINST EACH OTHER, THEY CAUSE THE GROUND TO SHAKE. THE PLACES THEY RUB ARE CALLED *FAULTS*, AND THE MOTION ON THE FAULT LINES IS WHAT WE CALL EARTHQUAKES.

LUCKILY, SCIENTIST CHARLES FRANCIS RICHTER DEVISED A 10-POINT SCALE THAT HELPS MEASURE HOW INTENSE THE MOVEMENT OF THE TECTONIC PLATES GETS. THE SHAKIER THE SEISMOGRAPH LINE ON THE *RICHTER SCALE*, THE WORSE THE EARTHQUAKE.

AND IT LOOKS LIKE THIS NEXT ONE IS GETTING PRETTY BAD! LET'S GET OUT OF HERE!

OH NO! I'M LOSING MY BEAUTIFUL GEM!

LET IT GO, MAN! IT'S NOT WORTH IT!

I KNOW IT ISN'T. I JUST LIKE MAKING A BIG DEAL OUT OF THINGS!

RUMBLE! RUMBLE!

THE Richter Richard Scale

Explore the phases of the Richter Scale with Mr. Dad's personal take on earthquake magnitudes!

RICHTER SCALE READING OF:

 ZZZZZZZZZZZZZZZZ!

0-1
Quakes not felt by people

2-3
Minor quakes with slight shaking

 AH, WHAT A PLEASANT DAY.

4-5
Moderate quakes . . . Find cover!

 I'VE HAD BURPS THAT WERE SHAKIER THAN THIS.

 I TAKE IT ALL BACK! I'M SO SCARED!

6-8
Major quakes with all buildings in danger

9-10
A great earthquake with major destruction

 THAT'S IT! I'M MOVING TO NEW HAMPSHIRE, WHERE NOTHING EVER HAPPENS!

DO-IT-YOURSELF EXPERIMENT: SUGAR CRYSTALS!

TASTE THE SWEET SUCCESS OF MAKING YOUR OWN MINERALS

WHAT YOU'LL NEED:

- 3 cups of table sugar
- A clean glass jar
- A pencil or pen
- A piece of string (not nylon!)
- Food coloring
- Regular kitchen items like measuring cups, pots, and spoons

WHAT YOU DO:

- Cut a piece of string long enough to hang in the jar without touching the bottom, and then tie it to your pencil.
- Bring 1 cup of water to a boil, and then slowly stir in your sugar until all of it dissolves completely.
- Add food coloring to the mixture, and then pour it into your jar.
- Balance your pencil across the jar so the string dips into the water. Then set it aside for a day to watch your crystal form!

46

MAKE A HYPOTHESIS:

→ What do you think will happen?

TEST YOUR HYPOTHESIS:

→ How big was your piece of sugar crystal? Would more sugar make it bigger, or would it ruin the experiment? Why?

→ Sugar is a naturally occuring chemical compound that shares an orderly crystalline structure with many minerals. What shape do you think its molecules have? Draw your own version!

Anais's Favorite Scientists

FACTOID 1:

Marie Curie is one of the most famous scientists of all time, known for her work in both physics and chemistry. She discovered the elements polonium and radium, and she coined the term "radioactivity." But did you know that she also had a scientist daughter?

FORGET ISAAC NEWTON AND CHARLES RICHTER! THESE ARE THE SCIENTISTS I WANNA BE LIKE WHEN I GROW UP!

Her daughter Irene Curie-Joliot followed in Marie's footsteps by experimenting with artificial radioactivity, and made new discoveries about the structure of atoms. When Irene won the Nobel Prize in chemistry in 1935, it made the mother/daughter pair the first parent/child winners of the prize in history.

FACTOID 2:

In 1811, then eleven-year-old Mary Anning dug up parts of a prehistoric reptile called the ichthyosaurus near her home in England (her brother thought it was a crocodile). For the next several decades, she was a professional fossil hunter, finding the remains of beasts like the pterodactyl and contributing to our understanding of ancient sea life.

FACTOID 3:

Rosalind Franklin took the first-ever photograph of the double-helix structure of DNA in 1952. But before she could publish her discovery, two other scientists in her lab used her picture to help them win a Nobel Prize in medicine. Today, we consider her the true pioneer of DNA research.

SHOW 'EM WHO'S BOSS!

CHAPTER 5
BIOLOGY

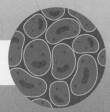

FOR OUR NEXT SCIENTIFIC STEP, WE'VE GOT TO EXAMINE THE BIOLOGICAL PROCESSES OF LIVING ORGANISMS.

BUT CAN EVEN THE MOST INTREPID SCIENTIST SURVIVE AN IN-DEPTH LOOK AT A BEING WHOSE EVERY ORIFICE HAS BEEN KNOWN TO EMIT NOXIOUS GASES AT ANY POSSIBLE MOMENT?

YOU KNOW, I CAN HEAR YOU, AND WORDS HURT!

BUT GUMBALL, WE'RE ABOUT TO EMBARK ON THE STUDY OF LIFE ITSELF!

WHAT BETTER FRONTIER TO EXPLORE NEXT THAN *BIOLOGY*?

DARWIN, TODAY I'VE SURVIVED EXPLOSIONS, STINKY FORMULAS, SPACE FLIGHT, A MOUNTAIN CRASH, AND AN EARTHQUAKE. AND NOW YOU BRING ME *BACK TO SCHOOL*?

CARTOON CHARACTERS HAVE NO BIOLOGY. WE'RE ALL INK AND IMAGINATION AND CAFFEINE-FUELED DREAMS.

INSANE?

I DOUBT THERE'S EVEN ANY BONES IN MY BODY. IT'S PROBABLY JUST A BUNCH OF RUBBER BANDS HELD TOGETHER BY BUBBLE GUM, WITH BLUE DYE TO MAKE ME MORE APPEALING.

EXTREME STRETCHINESS & SQUISHINESS

POSSIBLY FILLED WITH JELLY BEANS

THAT MIGHT JUST BE THE SMARTEST THING YOU'VE SAID SINCE WE STARTED, GUMBALL, BUT THERE ARE STILL PLACES WHERE WE ELMORIANS FIT INTO THE BIG WORLD OF SCIENCE.

YOU'RE A CAT, AND I'M A FISH WITH LEGS, AND ANIMALS LIKE US ARE ALWAYS EASY TO CLASSIFY IF YOU ONLY USE . . .

TAXNOMIC RANKINGS!!

THIS SYSTEM SHOWS HOW COMPLEX LIVING ORGANISMS ARE RELATED TO EACH OTHER.

A LIVING THING'S **KINGDOM** CLASSIFIES WHETHER IT'S PART OF A GROUP LIKE ANIMALS, PLANTS, FUNGI, OR BACTERIA.

DOMAIN

KINGDOM

FURTHER DOWN THE CHAIN, **CLASS** AND **ORDER** HELP US FIGURE OUT WHAT SPECIFIC KIND OF ORGANISM WE'RE TALKING ABOUT, SUCH AS MAMMALS OR FISH OR MOSS OR ALGAE.

PHYLUM

CLASS

AND THE FINAL TWO RANKS—**GENUS** AND **SPECIES**—TELL US THE SCIENTIFIC LABEL FOR A SPECIFIC ORGANISM.

ORDER

FAMILY

COMBINING THE LATIN WORDS FOR EACH OF THOSE GROUPS GETS YOU WHAT SCIENTISTS CALL YOUR **BINOMIAL NAME**.

GENUS

SPECIES

WHAT? I'VE GOT ENOUGH NAMES ON MY HANDS WITH **GUMBALL TRISTOPHER WATTERSON**, THANKS VERY MUCH.

CREATE AN ELMORIAN

As Gumball and Darwin avoid getting detention, come up with a brand-new Elmore Junior High School student. Pick one of the three scientific names Gumball created, and draw a character that best fits the feel:

*SWAGEST HAGGUS   * DODGERI DAREO   * KICKIGI MAXIMUS

I DON'T SEE PRINCIPAL BROWN ANYWHERE! DID WE LOSE HIM?

I DON'T KNOW, BUT I THINK WE PICKED UP SOMEONE EVEN STRANGER!

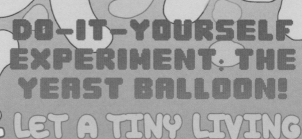

DO-IT-YOURSELF EXPERIMENT: THE YEAST BALLOON!

LET A TINY LIVING ORGANISM PUMP YOU UP

EVEN THE TINIEST OF LIVING ORGANISMS UNDERGO BASIC BIOLOGICAL PROCESSES—LIKE YEAST! THE SINGLE-CELLED MICROFUNGUS WE USE TO BAKE BREAD BREATHES LIKE ANYTHING ELSE.

SURE, BUT I BET I CAN HOLD MY BREATH FOR LONGER THAN IT CAN!

WHAT YOU'LL NEED:

- → An empty water bottle
- → A balloon (not Alan)
- → A packet of yeast
- → Warm water
- → Some sugar

BE CAREFUL WITH THAT YEAST, HUH? IT COULD BE MY DISTANT COUSIN!

WHAT YOU DO:

→ Blow your balloon up several times so it's nice and stretchy.

→ Fill your water bottle up with about 1.25 inches of warm water.

→ Pour in your packet of yeast and swirl it around until it dissolves in the water. Then add 1 teaspoon of sugar.

→ Quickly stretch the mouth of the balloon over the top of the bottle so it creates a seal.

→ Watch the yeast respirate and inflate the balloon!

MAKE A HYPOTHESIS

→ What do you think will happen?

TEST YOUR HYPOTHESIS:

→ How quickly did the balloon inflate? Was it as fast as you expected?

→ What happens if you use more water, more yeast, or more sugar in the experiment? What's the best combination to inflate the balloon fastest?

Biological Processes Crossword

WE ALL DO SOME FORM OF THESE THINGS IN ORDER TO LIVE. DON'T LET THE GROSSNESS SCARE YOU OFF!

CLUES:

1. How animals like Gumball and Darwin breathe oxygen
2. When you increase in size due to eating, sleeping, and just living, man
3. If you get all sweaty because you're working out or because Penny's around
4. How a body breaks down food into energy, tissue, and waste (that means poop!)
5. When an organism breaks down chemically, like milk turning into stinky cheese
6. When a living thing changes from one form into another
7. The way plants, like Leslie, turn light, water, and CO_2 into energy and oxygen
8. How organisms duplicate or re-create their kind (hint: ask your parents)

CHAPTER 6

ELECTRICITY

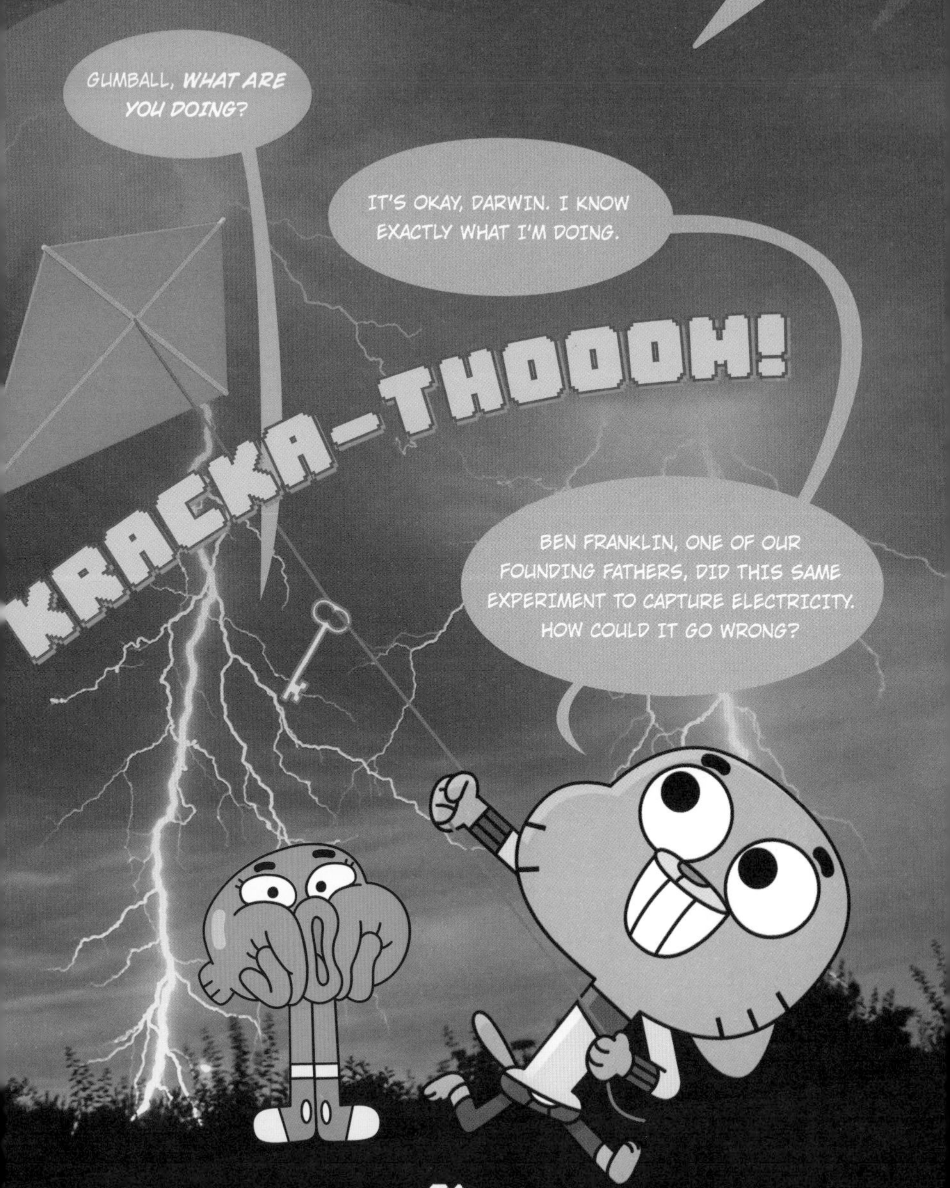

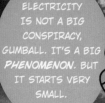

ELECTRICITY IS NOT A BIG CONSPIRACY, GUMBALL. IT'S A BIG *PHENOMENON.* BUT IT STARTS VERY SMALL.

ELECTRICITY STARTS WHEN ANY FORM OF MATTER HAS TOO MANY OF THE TEENY-TINY PARTICLES CALLED *PROTONS* AND *ELECTRONS.*

IF SOMETHING HAS MORE PROTONS, IT IS *POSITIVELY CHARGED.* IF IT HAS MORE ELECTRONS, IT'S *NEGATIVELY CHARGED.*

YOU HAVE NO IDEA HOW MANY NEGATIVE CHARGES I HAVE HANGING AROUND ME.

HEY, I WAS JUST MINDING MY OWN BUSINESS OVER HERE!

POSITIVELY AND NEGATIVELY CHARGED PARTICLES ARE ATTRACTED TO EACH OTHER. AND WHEN THEY GET CLOSE, ELECTRONS CAN JUMP FROM ONE THING TO THE OTHER.

THAT'S WHY YOU CAN SHOCK A FRIEND WITH STATIC ELECTRICITY.

ZAK!!

OW!

SOME MATERIALS— LIKE RUBBER— RESIST ELECTRICAL CHARGES. WE CALL THESE INSULATORS. THIS IS WHY YOU CAN BUILD UP A CHARGE IN YOUR HAIR BY RUBBING A BALLOON ON YOUR HEAD.

NO, ALAN. WE DON'T NEED YOU TO DEMONSTRATE.

AWWWWWW.

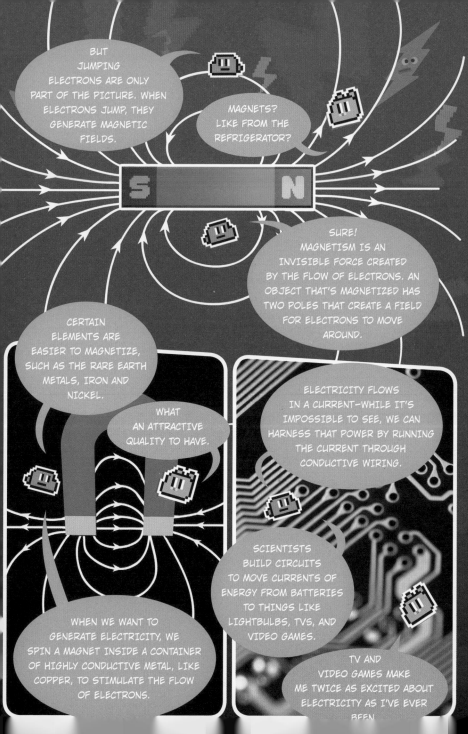

DO-IT-YOURSELF EXPERIMENT: MAKE A MAGNET

WHAT YOU'LL NEED:

→ A few different types of household nails
→ At least one refrigerator magnet
→ Some paper clips

WHAT TO DO:

→ Take a magnet and run it along the length of a nail several times as if you were peeling a carrot.
→ Test the nail's tip to see if it will pick up the paper clips.
→ Repeat with the different kinds of nails.

MAGNETS ARE AMAZING THINGS. BEYOND HELPING US GATHER ELECTRICITY, THEY CAN REORDER THE ATOMS OF CERTAIN KINDS OF METAL TO MAGNETIZE THEM AS WELL. TRY IT OUT YOURSELF!

MAKE A HYPOTHESIS:

→ What do you think will happen?

TEST YOUR HYPOTHESIS:

→ Were you able to magnetize every nail? If not, what do you think was different about them?
→ Make a prediction and then try the following: Use a stack of multiple magnets on a nail, or connect your magnets to the base of the nail. Can the nail still move the paper clips?

Complete the Circuit

INSTRUCTIONS:

Poor Bobert will power down unless he gets a recharge. But Gumball can't tell which of these three wires will connect his pal to the battery and complete the circuit. Trace each wire to find which one will give him a charge.

SHOCKING ART

Good Job! Bobert has gained so much electrical energy that he's able to upgrade to his awesome combat mode. From lasers to propellers and beyond, what elements do you think a mighty robot can use? Draw them in below!

DO-IT-YOURSELF EXPERIMENT: THE ELECTRIFYING POTATO CLOCK

HARNESS THE POWER OF NATURE IN THE PALM OF YOUR HAND

YOU'D BE CRAZY TO TRY TO ELECTRIFY A KITE LIKE GUMBALL DID, BUT YOU CAN MAKE YOUR OWN POTATO-POWERED CLOCK WITH SOME COMMON ITEMS FROM THE HARDWARE STORE.

YOU BETTER HOPE THE POTATO YOU USE IS COMMON, TOO, BECAUSE IDAHO GIVES TOO MUCH BACK TALK!

12:00

WHAT YOU'LL NEED:

Y'ALL ARE JUST JEALOUS BECAUSE YOU COULDN'T EVEN POWER A PENLIGHT!

- ⇢ A potato
- ⇢ 2 pennies or copper nails
- ⇢ 2 galvanized nails
- ⇢ 3 (8-inch) jump wires with alligator clips on each end
- ⇢ A digital clock that runs on one battery alone

WHAT YOU DO:

⇥ Get an adult to help you cut the potato in half and set the pieces down on your table so they sit cut-side down.

⇥ Remove the battery from the clock so you can see the places in the battery compartment labeled positive (⊕) and negative (⊖).

⇥ Stick one of the pennies (or copper nails) and one galvanized nail into each of the potato halves. Be sure to place the penny and nail far apart from each other.

⇥ Take your first jump wire and use its clips to connect the penny in one potato half to the metal in the battery compartment's positive terminal.

⇥ Take your second jump wire and connect the galvanized nail in your other potato half to the negative terminal.

⇥ Use the third jump wire to connect the remaining nail and penny to each other. This will complete the circuit and start the clock!

MAKE A HYPOTHESIS

⇥ What do you think will happen?

TEST YOUR HYPOTHESIS:

⇥ Did the clock turn on? If not, check that you're connecting the wires in the right formation. The hydrogen ions from the potato's phosphoric acid will only create electricity with the right flow.

⇥ How long do you think the clock will run? Time it and see!

⇥ Do you think a lemon will power the clock longer or shorter than a potato? Try it and compare your results!

Real-Life "Mad" Scientists

MWA-HA-HA-HA! NOW WITH THE FULL FORCE OF SCIENTIFIC KNOWLEDGE AT MY COMMAND, I'LL FINALLY HAVE THE POWER TO SHOW THEM ALL HOW WRONG THEY WERE TO LAUGH AT ME!

GET REAL, GUMBALL! THERE'S NO SUCH THING AS MAD SCIENTISTS BENT ON CONQUERING THE WORLD. BUT SOME OF THE GREATEST SCIENTISTS EVER WERE CALLED "MAD" FOR THE WACKY PATHS THEY TOOK TO GREAT DISCOVERIES!

FACTOID 1:

Though he never became as famous as his former mentor Thomas Edison, physicist and electrical engineer **NIKOLA TESLA** broke strange new ground in his career. After pioneering alternating-current electricity, Tesla built giant broadcast towers to try to transmit energy through the air. He created **135-foot**-long bolts of artificial lightning, proposed an antiaircraft weapon some called a death ray, and fell in love with a pigeon. While he was largely overlooked in his lifetime, today we credit him with technology that brought us modern conveniences like generators and the internet.

FACTOID 2:

The child of famed poet Lord Byron and a math-minded mother, **ADA LOVELACE** described her work as "poetical science." In the early **1800s**, she traveled around Europe making friends with artists like Charles Dickens and doing complicated math for scientists like computer pioneer Charles Babbage. Lovelace's early work writing algorithms for Babbage's "analytical engine" made her the very first computer programmer.

FACTOID 3:

For decades in the early **1900s**, botanist **GEORGE WASHINGTON CARVER** served as a researcher and teacher at the famed Tuskegee Institute in Alabama. But he is most famous for finding over three hundred things that could be made out of peanuts, including glue, instant coffee, makeup, shoe polish, and shaving cream.

FACTOID 4:

Some people thought primatologist **JANE GOODALL** was weird because she went to Africa to live with chimpanzees when she was only twenty-six, and some criticize her for naming her chimp subjects instead of giving them scientific numbers. But by getting so close to the animals, Goodall was able to learn more about primate behavior than ever before, including how chimps create a society, eat meat, and adopt orphans.

FACTOID 5:

Though she was best known as a famous Hollywood actress, **HEDY LAMARR** moonlighted as an inventor. She created things like a new kind of traffic light, a carbonated soda drink, and most importantly, a "frequency hopping" method for sending radio signals. It's this last invention that became the basis for how Internet WiFi works.

YOU MEAN THE REASON I CAN SURF THE WEB ON MY PHONE IS BECAUSE OF A MOVIE STAR?

SCIENTISTS ARE WORTH A LOT MORE THAN THEIR GOOD LOOKS, GUMBALL.

Scientific Theory

Don't let Gumball have all the fun! Create your own theory
for a scientific issue that's every bit as weird.

1. THE PROBLEM I WANT TO SOLVE IS . . .

....

....

2. MY EXPERIMENT WOULD INVOLVE . . .

....

....

....

....

3. BUT THE REAL CRAZY PART HAPPENS WHEN . . .

....

....

....

....

....

....

I THOUGHT MY IDEAS
WERE WEIRD, BUT YOU GUYS ARE
STRAIGHT-UP NUTS!

CHAPTER 7

FINAL EXAM

NAME: GUMBALL WATTERSON

1. The force that holds planet Earth together is called what?
 EARTHQUAKE GLUE

2. How old is planet Earth?
THE SAME AGE AS MISS SIMIAN (OLDER THAN DIRT)

3. What layer of Earth comes between the crust and the core?
THE SEAT BELT

4. What element creates light when energized in glass tubing?
TUBANIUM?

5. A molecule is negatively charged if it has too many what?
BAD DAYS THIS WEEK

6. The parts of the Earth's lithosphere that cause earthquakes are called what?
GRANNY JOJO'S FINE CHINA

I'VE ABOUT HAD IT. IF SOMEONE DOESN'T SHOW THAT THEY LEARNED SOMETHING FROM THIS BOOK SOON, YOU'LL ALL BE GIVEN DETENTION . . . FOR ETERNITY!

7. In the taxonomic rankings, what comes between phylum and order?
ANARCHY!

8. How high does the Richter Scale go?
ONE QUADRILLION

9. What's the most prominent element in Earth's atmosphere?
CAR EXHAUST

10. Metamorphic rocks combine elements of what two things?
HIP-HOP AND SMOOTH JAZZ

11. What is the term for your scientific name based on genus and species?
BIONIC

12. All the different ecosystems of Earth combine to make one what?
BIG MESS

13. Molecules created when two elements combine are called what?
KISSING COUSINS

14. What's the term for when Earth's atmosphere pushes against an object in motion?
BLOWHARD

15. The flow of electricity always travels in what?
A SINGLE-FILE LINE

16. The only way to prove that a scientific theory is true is to do what?
YELL IT WAY LOUDER THAN THE OTHER GUY

17. What are three basic biological processes?
CHILLING, RAPPING, AND THUMB-WRESTLING

18. The order of elements in the periodic table is determined by what?
WHO HAD THE MOST CALLERS TO THEIR 1-800 NUMBER

Page 17 Answers:

1. Carbon dioxide
2. Sugar
3. Chalk
4. Vitamin C
5. Aspirin
6. Borax

Pages 32–33 Pop Quiz Answers:

1. Water
2. Friction
3. Matter
4. Hypothesis
5. Noble gases
6. Proton, neutron, and electron
7. Hydrogen
8. 25,000 miles per hour
9. A force acts upon it

Page 42 Maze Solution

Gumball's Gem Hunt

INSTRUCTIONS:
Dig deep into the crust or the earth with gumball as he hunts for precious gemstones!

42

Page 60

```
                                    4D
                                     I
              1R                      G
               E          7P          E
               S           H          S
              2G           O          T
              8R E P R O D U C T I O N     5F
               O           O          N     E
               W           S                R
               T           Y                M
               H           N                E
                           T                N
                           H                T
                       3P E R S P I R A T I O N
                           I                T
              6M E T A M O R P H O S I S     I
                                            O
                                            N
```

Page 67 Complete The Circuit Maze Solution

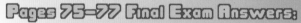

Pages 75-77 Final Exam Answers:

1. Gravity
2. Four and a half billion years old
3. The mantle
4. Neon
5. Electrons
6. Tectonic plates
7. Class
8. It goes to 10
9. Nitrogen
10. Igneous and sedimentary rocks
11. Binomial
12. Biosphere
13. Chemical compounds
14. Air resistance
15. Currents
16. Devise a test
17. Breathing, digesting, growing, sweating, etc.
18. Their atomic number